Sir Dana: A Knight
As told by his trusty armor

MUCH TRAINING AND STRENGTH DOES IT TAKE...

Words and pictures by
Dana Fradon

E. P. DUTTON • NEW YORK

to Amy and Pat

Published in the United States by E. P. Dutton,
2 Park Avenue, New York, N.Y. 10016,
a division of NAL Penguin Inc.

Published simultaneously in Canada by
Fitzhenry & Whiteside Limited, Toronto

Designer: Alice Lee Groton

Printed in Hong Kong by South China Printing Co.
First Edition   W   10 9 8 7 6 5 4 3 2 1

Library of Congress Cataloging-in-Publication Data

Fradon, Dana.
    Sir Dana: a knight, as told by his trusty armor/written and
illustrated by Dana Fradon.—1st ed.   p.   cm.
    Summary: A class of students visiting the medieval room of a mu-
seum ask questions of a suit of armor on display there about knights
and the civilization in which they lived.   ISBN 0-525-44424-6
    1. Knights and knighthood—Juvenile literature.   2. Civilization,
Medieval—Juvenile literature.   3. Questions and answers—Juvenile
literature. [1. Knights and knighthood.   2. Civilization,
Medieval.   3. Questions and answers.]   I. Title.   CR4513.F73
1988   929.7—dc19   88-3968   CIP   AC

A thank-you to Marcy Mankoff of Kids America radio, who was the first person to address the author as Sir Dana. And thanks also to Eleanor Bancroft, who found me a nineteenth-century copy of Froissart. Its title page reads: "Chronicles of England, France, Spain, and the Adjoining Countries, From the Latter Part of the Reign of Edward II to the Coronation of Henry IV, by Sir John Froissart.* Translated by Thomas Johnes, Esq."

---

*He was not, to our knowledge, a Sir, and John stands for *Jean.*

When you come to a colored dot in the text, find the
same-colored dot below for a little more information.

In the medieval room of a great museum, Miss Quincy and her class are looking at the armor worn by a knight six hundred years ago.

The armor is so real it seems as if there must still be someone inside. The children wonder about him. Was he a mean or a gentle knight? Did he ever get scared? Was the armor heavy to wear?

"Imagine what this armor could tell us if it could talk," Miss Quincy says to her students. The armor remains silent, of course, but a museum guard does speak up.

The armor quivers ever so slightly
and with much clynkyn● and clanging . . .

● Medieval for *"Here we go again!"*
● Medieval for *clinking*

. . . SPEAKS! But in hard-to-understand medieval English.

Who wore you? one of the children asked.

"I will tell you a little about us—I mean *him*. Sir Dana of Domania was the knight who wore me. You won't find him mentioned in history books, but what I tell you about Sir Dana and his fellow knights and medieval life is true. If you ever read the chronicles written in the fourteenth century, you will see that they support my words.

"Sir Dana and I were comrades in adventure six hundred years ago. Sir Dana was a warrior on horseback. Without my protection, he would have accomplished little. And without Sir Dana, I would be but a heap of rusted iron—sore expensive iron to be sure. I could cost one-quarter of a petty knight's ● yearly wage. Little wonder, for my hauberk ● alone was made of some two hundred thousand tiny iron rings linked together, and it took one skilled ironworker two months to make. The king of Domania gave me to Sir Dana, along with a horse and weapons, when he knighted him.

● A young knight without much money

● A shirt of chain mail

"Sir Dana was a valiant warrior. Not many serious dents did my helmet or pieces of plate receive in battle, and the few received were quickly repaired and I was reshined. Only a successful knight could afford to have a servant constantly polishing his armor. To save money and time, some knights blued their armor with heat, others blackened it with heat and oil, and a few painted it. My hauberk and leg mail were shaken in a bag with vinegar and sand or sawdust to clean off the rust, and then lightly oiled.

"But by my faith! Enough of myself!

"Sir Dana was born on Averil 14, 1331, in the tiny kingdom of Domania, on the Dordogne River, between Beynac and Sarlat. His father was a very rich knight who held the noble title Lord. This made Sir Dana a member of the noble class. Thus it was his duty to protect the king and the other members of the royal family from their many enemies. And, I might add, to protect the castles and lands that belonged to Sir Dana's own family from enemy knights and nobles who might try to steal them.

"Domania fought alongside the French in a war against England that lasted over one hundred years, from 1337 to 1453. Sir Dana spent almost his entire knighthood fighting this war, defending French lands against English kings and nobles who wanted to rule them.

IRELAND
LONDON
ENGLAND
ENGLISH CHANNEL
Normand
Brittany
BEYNAC
BORDEAUX
Gascony
Foix
PYRENEES MOUNTAINS

● Medieval for *April*

● A made-up name for a real geographic area in what is now the Dordogne region of France

"Sir Dana never married. His one love, Lady Elizabeth, died during the great pestilence.

"A gentle person Sir Dana was. During the pestilence, when millions of people died, he was among those who helped the sick. He made them comfortable, gave them liquids and food, bathed their sores, and when they died, he administered the last rites of the Catholic church. Many priests had died or fled the pestilence, so ordinary citizens—even women—were sometimes allowed to administer the rites.

"Wise and prudent Sir Dana was. Unlike many of his less educated companions, he spoke French and English and could read French and Latin. He wrote in French. Sir Dana even had a personal library of a dozen or so books—a lot for that time. He enjoyed poetry and spoke with wit and charm, a trait much valued at court."

● The Black Death, bubonic plague

Why did Sir Dana become a knight?

"Truth to tell, as the son of a knight, no thought was ever given to his being anything else. From the day of his birth, he was prepared for this lifelong task. As a child, Sir Dana played games that developed his physical skills.

"Using toy wooden swords, he and his friends pretended they were knights.

"They walked on stilts.

"They played catch with a ball made of leather or cloth stuffed with almost anything. Wool was best. It was light and held its shape.

"Sometimes they would hit the ball over a net or a raised mound of earth with a gloved hand.

"Not all of his amusements developed Sir Dana's physical skills. He collected and played with toy wooden knights. Sometimes he and his sister played with a little cart drawn by a live mouse. He also played checkers, chess, backgammon, marbles, and horseshoes.

"Then, at age eight, as was the custom, he was taken by his parents to a baron's castle some thirty leagues● to the east, along with other boys from noble families. For the next six years, this would be his home, his school, and his training ground for knighthood.

"Tutors taught him to read Latin and French. He studied algebra, geometry, logic,● and of course the Bible.

"Outside in the fields he practiced riding so that someday he would be a superb horseman. He practiced with his lance at the quintain● and grew strong swinging the five-to-twelve-pound broadsword and the mace, and pulling on the taut strings of the longbow.

"At age fourteen he left the castle—a squire."

● An inexact measurement that can be one, two, or three miles
● The art of reasoning—how to debate
● Something like a big punching bag

What's a squire?

"A squire was a knight's assistant, his apprentys, you might say. A squire followed his knight on the way to battle, leading the knight's courser● and caring for his equipment. The knight rode his palfrey.●

"For the first few years, squires did not take part in battle. But as they grew older and stronger, many squires fought alongside their knights as equals, with much valor, and did great mischief● to the enemy. The great English knight Sir John Chandos met his death at the hands of a strong, experienced squire.

THERE MUST BE AN EASIER WAY TO GET TO BE A KNIGHT.

● Medieval for *apprentice*
● Battle horse
● Regular riding horse
● Damage

"Some men chose to remain squires their entire lives. Expensive it was to become a knight.  Living as an assistant to a rich lord or successful knight was often as good as being one."

● A great lord needed to supply a new knight only with a horse, armor, and weapons. The new knight often had to pay for lavish feasting and ceremonies himself.

● Woof!

How old was Sir Dana when he became a knight?

"Sir Dana was twenty-one, the age most squires became knights. But many a squire was made a knight while still a teenager.

"On the other hand, the great French knight Sir Bertrand du Guesclin—the Tenth Worthy●—did not become a knight until he was thirty-five.

"Mind you this: A king could confer knighthood on almost anyone he wished—at any age. Many a rich merchant bought the honor of knighthood with money. Some poor but able foot soldiers earned it on the field of battle through their bravery. The nobles, of course, were exceedingly wroth● at this backward entry into their class, but they could not entirely halt it.

"Squire Dana became a knight, and received the title Sir, in a ceremony many centuries old. Having taken a purifying bath the night before to cleanse him of his sins, he dressed all in white to signify his purity. He vowed to serve and

● The tenth greatest knight of all time, so deemed by his countrymen
● Medieval for *upset*

defend God, the king of Domania, his fellow knights, womanhood, and the weak. And at all times to act in a just, gentlemanly, and chivalrous manner.

"Then the king girded him—fastened a sword and belt around Squire Dana's waist. Riding spurs were attached to his boots.

"After that an odd, *very* odd, thing happened. The king delivered the buffet, an open-handed blow to the cheek. Sometimes it was merely symbolic, and sometimes it was powerful enough to send a knight reeling.

"The buffet ended the ceremony. Some say its purpose was to make sure the young knight never forgot his vows."

BUFFET!

● Medieval for *slap*

Could a girl be a knight? Was Joan of Arc a knight?

"No! Why, a knight was not even supposed to ride a mare! It was believed that females had no place on the battlefield. However, here and there, women did go to war—and as leaders, too. Queen Philippa of England was said to have urged her troops to fight manfully at the Battle of Neville's Cross. She prevented a Scottish invasion, while her husband, King Edward III, and most of his knights were across the English Channel fighting the French. And the countess of Montfort led the defense of her castle and lands when her husband was a prisoner of the French. She was said to possess the courage of a man and the heart of a lion!

"I know not directly of Joan of Arc. She died, burned at the stake, in 1431. Sir Dana would have been one hundred years old by then. A great leader, she wore full armor as she led her troops against the English. A saint she became, but not a knight."

Explain royalty and nobility.

"The royal class was highest of all the medieval classes of people. The king was its head. He ruled the land and was an almost godlike figure to his subjects. His wife, sons, daughters, brothers, and other relatives were the royal family—the queen, princes, princesses, and dukes of the kingdom. Now, how does this great good fortune first favor such a family? Ho! By force of arms, usually. Conquer another king, place yourself on his throne, and a new royal family is born.

"Next came the noble class—the defenders of the kingdom—the barons, earls, lords, and knights. Many nobles were almost as powerful as the king and could gather armies of knights to make private wars—on each other. Nobles sometimes married into royal families, blurring the distinction between the two classes.

"Below royalty and nobility were the gentry—rich landowners, merchants, bankers—often richer than some nobility and often able to buy their way into the noble class. Then came the common folk—weavers, fishmongers, grocers, shoemakers, and so on. And last came the lowly peasants, who tilled the soil for their masters for precious little reward.

"The medieval church had much power and influence in all these classes. Knights believed deeply in God and the holy church, some knights less than others, but none were unbelievers. Prayers were said before entering battle; biblical quotations were etched on helmets. Sir John Chandos's surcoat, worn over his armor, was emblazoned with an image of the Virgin Mary."

Were knights rich?

"Some were and some were not. Some who were great lords owned dozens of castles, much land, and many villages and employed thousands of peasants, servants, craftsmen, and other knights.

"Others owned only their armor, weapons, and horse.

"But the poorest knight was far richer than most peasants, who did not earn in a year the price of a knight's horse and equipment."

● Medieval for *money*

● Medieval for *hay*

What were Sir Dana's favorite sports?

"Ho! He liked wrestling, running, archery, and swimming. Even more he liked to hunt with his trained female peregrine falcon. It was a sport that also put food on his table. Sir Dana would release his falcon, and she would fly at the prey, kill it, and then return for her reward, a small tidbit of meat or fowl, sometimes from the kill itself. Why did he use a female falcon and not a male? Well, the female is bigger and more ferocious.

"Sir Dana also loved to hunt the wild beasts of the forests, with spear or bow and arrow, on horseback.

"His hunting parties included many friends, women among them, along with trained huntsmen to lead the party, servants, horn blowers, beaters, ● and dog handlers.

● Medieval for *falcon*

● The signal given to the bird to attack, not unlike "giddap" to a horse

● They make loud noises and scare the game out of hiding.

"Keen-scented dogs, mostly huge hounds, tracked the prey. They were trained to obey the horn blasts, which could be heard over their barking and baying, the thunder of hooves, and the hunters' excited cries. Soon the party might be feasting splendidly on the stag, the doe, the boar, or the wolf. Well, maybe not the wolf. He would just become a wolfskin coat or blanket.

"Sometimes arrows alone could not kill the ferocious boar. A brave, or perhaps foolhardy, knight would dismount and on foot strike the animal dead with his longsword. Sometimes, alas, the beast finished off the knight. This is true.

"And then there was the greatest of medieval sports: the joust, also called the tournament or tilt.

"On a smooth green field of grass, lined with colorful tents and spectators, and perhaps a king in attendance, many knights gathered to test their prowess with the lance. One against one, mounted and in decorated tournament armor, they would eye each other from opposite sides of the field, waiting for a signal from a herald.  Then—for their horses were huge—they charged at a lumbering gallop. Each knight held a lance in his right hand, a shield in his left. The reins of their horses hung loose. Only pressure from the knees and a shift of weight in the saddles directed the mounts. The object was to unhorse● or unhelm● the opponent with one stunning blow. And, above all, to do it with courage and honor. Many were

● Heralds were officials with many duties, among them running tournaments.
● Knock off horse
● Knock helmet off

sorely injured and some even killed, though killing was not the purpose of the joust. The lances were usually, but not always, peace lances, or dull tipped.

"Shields and armor were pierced. Lances might shatter and real sparks fly. The noise could be deafening. So scary was it all that sometimes, after running a few lances,  a horse would simply refuse to budge. Ha! Smart horse.

"In some tournaments, winners were entitled to the loser's horse, armor, and weapons, worth much money. Others, such as the great tournament at Saint Inglevere, which lasted almost a month during a truce in the Hundred Years War, were for honor and sport alone. There, three French knights challenged any and all of the knights of England to joust. Over forty knights took up the challenge. Both sides acquitted themselves well."

● Each single charge was also called a lance.

What is chivalry?

"It was a code, the rules and values of knighthood, written and unwritten, going back at least to the ninth-century Anglo-Saxon king Alfred. It included a devotion to duty, fair play on the battlefield, honesty, good manners, and bravery. Also kindness toward the weak, respect for women, courtesy, generosity, and gentleness toward everyone. Above all, it pledged the knight to serve God. By Saint Denis! Not bad values, even for today, eh?

"Sad to say, these rules were much broken. Knights often killed needlessly. Ho! Is killing ever but needless? Chivalrous behavior was often forgotten in dealings with peasants, religious minorities, or anybody a knight disliked.

"If a captured knight promised to pay a ransom in exchange for being allowed to return home unharmed, he would almost always keep his word.

"If a king granted safe passage through his country to certain of the enemy—as during peace talks—his subjects were expected to honor his word.

"In a battle of the Hundred Years War, the blind king of Bohemia, showing much bravery and noble spirit, spoke to his several attendants. 'Gentlemen, friends, and brethren-at-arms—as I am blind, I request of you to lead me into battle that I may strike one stroke with my sword.' With their reins all tied together so they would not be separated, the king and his comrades rode into the fierce fray. The next morning they were found dead, still honorably tied together.

"If a knight broke a rule in a tournament, he dishonored himself and his comrades. For instance, on each charge of a joust, one or both knights could be violently unhelmed—at the least. It was an explosive shock to have a fully laced helmet ripped from your head. Sir Reginald de Roye, tilting with Sir John Holland, attempted to soften this blow by fastening his helmet with but one slim thong. Thus his helmet flew off easily when struck. Sir John's English comrades shouted, 'Ha! The French do not fight fair; why is not his helmet as well buckled on as Sir John Holland's? We say he is playing tricks.' They were sore put because they thought it was not chivalrous to seek clever, sneaky advantages.

"A friend of Sir Dana's, Sir Geoffrey de Charny, wrote three books on the meaning of chivalry, extending the code to include all men-at-arms, not just knights. His writings taught honor, compassion, moderation, cheerfulness, and above all the spirit of love. Sir Geoffrey was called the Perfect Knight, perhaps because he was not only a brave warrior but also a writer and philosopher."

Did knights have guns?

"No, not in Sir Dana's time. The bombard, a small early cannon that shot an iron, leather, or stone ball, did use a powder that exploded when it was sparked. But knights, who took pride only in direct personal combat, scorned its use. It wasn't considered chivalrous to strike the enemy from afar. So foot soldiers fired the bombard. Knights did appreciate that its loud *boom* frightened the enemies' horses. Little did they realize that this noisy weapon would someday make them—and their swords, lances, and maces—obsolete.

"I should add that knights also scorned the longbow because it, too, did not require hand-to-hand combat. Still, they always had much use for bowmen, or archers, in their armies—and for good reason! A bowman could with deadly accuracy shoot an arrow from his bow every twelve seconds, at distances up to three hundred yards. A veritable hailstorm of arrows could be rained down on the enemy.

"Ha! Some weapons were not much used because of their clumsy design. The two-ell● sword, too long to wield, and the twenty-five-pound mace, ● almost too heavy to lift, much less swing, were such weapons."

THANKS BE TO HEAVEN HIS WEAPON IS AS USELESS AS MINE!

THANKS BE TO HEAVEN HIS WEAPON IS AS USELESS AS MINE!

● An English ell was forty-five inches long.

● Most maces, hammers, and mallets weighed from four to ten pounds.

Could you be small and still be a knight?

"There were knights of every shape and size. Sir Bertrand du Guesclin, the Tenth Worthy, was short and heavy and ugly. Some called him a 'hog in armor'—not to his face, as he would be sorely vexed, and he was fearsome.

"Edward, the Black Prince, had a superb physique. Likewise that flower of English chivalry, Sir John Chandos, a man of great stature and strength, well made in all his limbs. And likewise Sir Dana, who was strongly made and not too much loaded with flesh.

"One day, in a field on the outskirts of a small town, Sir Dana saw two men on foot, battle-axes swinging, performing valiant deeds of arms, in a tilt ● to the death over some disagreement. One, an English knight, was small of stature, lightly made, and delicate in his form. The other, a French squire, was big, hardy, and strong, and much better formed in all his limbs. Ho! I won't tell you who won.

"But, big or small, knights had to be strong. How strong? Well, one cold evening, the count de Foix wanted firewood for a waning fire in an upstairs chimney. ● Sir Dana and a famous warrior, Ernauton d'Espaign, volunteered to carry it up.

"Outside, two donkeys were being led to the castle, both loaded with firewood. As a joke, each man picked up a donkey, firewood and all, carried it up twenty-four steps, and placed the entirety on the hearth, much to everyone's amusement. A true story it is. The writer Jean Froissart tells of this feat in his chronicles."

● A grudge duel with rules; one could only strike the body, not the arms or legs.

● Fireplace, one of many fireplaces in the castle

Tell us something about castles.

"A castle was both a home and a fortress—a mighty stone headquarters for waging war. Its many buildings were surrounded by a great wall, sometimes thirty feet thick and forty feet high or even higher, from which the lord of the castle could defend his lands or launch attacks.

"A castle took many years and hundreds of workmen to build. Often it was constructed at the edge of a sheer cliff plunging hundreds of feet to a river below. The cliff offered protection, since no enemy could attack from that side.

"During wars and battles, some castles housed more than a thousand knights and squires. And at all times a host of other occupants were present: armorers, pages, cooks, bakers, carpenters, grooms, stablehands, record keepers, a priest, a doctor, other craftsmen, even an occasional poet or artist or musician, and a steward to oversee it all.

"Some castles had secret escape tunnels, called mines, in case the castle was overrun by an enemy. Hand dug by miners and held up by heavy timbers, escape tunnels extended long distances underground and usually ended in a woods.

"A knight named Sir Walter de Passac once captured a castle in France and found no one there. He did not know about its escape tunnel and thought the people inside had disappeared by magic enchantment. Magic, indeed!"

What did Sir Dana eat?

"Sometimes, in war-torn areas burned bare of foliage, with all food animals frightened away, Sir Dana had little to eat. Once he ate grapes and vetches● for five days, supplemented only by pieces of stale bread, soggy from his horse's sweat, that he kept strapped behind his saddle. And some soggy oatmeal he had there too. This he mixed with water and baked into wafers, using a flat rock as a frying pan.

"At times his horse was so hungry it ate earth, heather, moss, and leaves—not exactly fresh grass and oats.

"But hold! Let us dwell on happier eating!

"I remember hearing of a small dinner given by the king of Domania. At midnight it began and lasted several hours. Fish, wildfowl, deer, stag, and wild boar were served. Sir Dana himself had killed the boar.

──────────────────────

● The vetch is a beanlike fruit.

"The boar was deliciously cooked in a stew sweetened with dates, raisins, and apricots from Eastern lands, served on peppermint rice. The bread was of wheat, baked with crushed rose petals. There were fruits and vegetables aplenty.

"Some foods were extra brightly colored with natural dyes made by boiling plants in water—dandelions for yellow, roses for red, and spinach for green. For dessert there were cakes and puddings sweetened with honey or fruit jams.

"Pages helped to serve. They were noble boys aged eight to twelve studying to be squires. They learned the good manners knights must have.

"It was a meal fit for a king."

Did they have pets in medieval times?

"Hunting dogs and falcons made fine pets. Sir Dana enjoyed taking his falcon to banquets and would tether her to the back of his chair during dinner.

"He once had a pet monkey, brought to Domania by North African spice traders. For a short while he kept a friend's trained bear—during which time he never removed his armor. Ho! I jest. Bears could be found almost everywhere in Europe. This bear came with a troupe of traveling entertainers, jugglers, and acrobats.

"Cats were not really pets. People kept them to catch rats and mice, but they were thought to be somewhat evil and could be treated cruelly.

"Fish were kept in ponds or in leather tanks right in the kitchen, not as pets but to eat. Still, Sir Dana enjoyed watching them swim about and letting them nibble his fingers.

"People named their pets. Sir Dana's dog was named Bodo. King Richard II of England named his favorite greyhound Math. And, harken ye this—Gaston Phoebus, the count de Foix, had over *sixteen hundred dogs*! I was told he took them with him everywhere. Their names were uh . . . um . . . oh, never mind."

I CAN'T BELIEVE IT!

BEWARE OF SIXTEEN HUNDRED DOGS

Did Sir Dana ever kill a dragon?

''I fear not. Had he felled a real, fire-breathing dragon with his broadsword, it would indeed have been exciting. But truth to tell, by Sir Dana's time all the dragons were gone, vanysshed,  extinct. Gone with the unicorn and flying horse. Maybe they never existed, but everybody, for certain, believed they did—and more!

Elves, ghosts, gnomes, giant serpents, gremlins, monsters, and other horrors of strange shape and form—half this, half that—were believed to lurk everywhere. Led by the all-powerful devel, deofel, deouel, devell, they went about committing their evil mischief.

● Medieval for *vanished*

● *Devil*—in medieval days, words could often be spelled many ways.

Did kings fight in battle?

"Kings often rode at the head of their troops, protected only by their own strong swords, trusted bodyguards, and by a strange and clever trick: duplicate kings. Doubles, copies, imitations—what you might today call clones—disguised to look like the real king and thus confuse the enemy.

"King John II of France once had nineteen duplicates at a battle. Still he was captured by the English—or was he? Who knows? Maybe it was a double.●

"A king captured alive was valuable because he could be held for ransom. A dead king could not be. That was really a ruler's best protection."

YOU DON'T FOOL ME. YOU'RE MY MASTER, SIR DANA.

● No, it wasn't a double. The real king *was* captured.

If someone was wounded in battle did anyone help?

"By Saint Denis! There were usually no doctors around! They would have been of little help in any case.

"A wounded leader—a prince, a duke, an earl, or a great knight—might be placed on his shield and moved to safety, protected by guards. If his wounds were not too great, his squire might stitch them up on the spot. Perhaps he would recover, perhaps he would not.

"For an ordinary knight who was wounded and could not escape the battle on his own, it was a different matter. If he was not rich enough to be captured and held for ransom, he could very well fall victim to a pillager. Pillagers were robbers and murderers who roamed the battlefield, sometimes almost under the horses' hooves, killing the wounded with long, slim daggers and stripping the unfortunate victims of their armor, clothing, and valuables.

"Death and pain were ever present. So also was the ability to endure them. I once saw a squire whose thighs had been pierced through by a lance continue to fight—it being the best medicine for survival. As long as he could wield his sword, he was still dangerous and could ward off pillagers.

"Alas, many wounds were mortal. Sometime after the Battle of Saint Salvin, during the Hundred Years War, I heard the writer Jean Froissart describe to Sir Dana how the great English knight Sir John Chandos died. No doctor could have helped *him*. This is the way it happened.

"He was approaching on foot. The ground was slippery from the morning's hoarfrost. His legs became entangled in his long robe and he made a tumble. A French squire, James de Saint Martin, thrust his lance into Sir John's accidentally open visor, hitting him below the eye. Sir John did not even see the stroke, for he had lost the eye on that side years before. He rolled over on the ground in agony and never uttered a word. He had received a death wound.

"Not very pretty, eh, my wurþy● children?

"Added to the perils of direct combat, knights in their forty-five to fifty-five pounds of poorly ventilated armor suffered heatstroke, suffocation, and heart failure. Sometimes these excellent horsemen were sorely injured by being thrown from their excited, rearing mounts.

● Medieval for *worthy*

"On occasion the dust churned up by the horses' hooves was so blindingly thick that knights coughed and spat mud. Most battles did not last long, and thousands might be killed or wounded in a few hours. After dark they sometimes fought by torchlight.

"Frankly, I prefer my present life in this peaceful museum."

Did knights ever get scared?

"Oh, my, yes. Often!

"Whether in battle with its terrible medley of spears and shields clashing and cries of 'Kill! Kill!' or in a joust, knights knew fear. Only the lunatyke● were unafraid.

"By a river that falls into the Thames near Oxford, England, the brave duke of Ireland waited to do battle with the dukes of York and Gloucester. While they were still some distance away he became much frightened. I have heard that he said, 'My courage entirely faileth me this day.' His fifteen-thousand-man army must have felt the same. They became panic stricken, quit their ranks, and fled in disorder. So great was their haste some were killed by riding over or into each other.

"By my faith! The entire countryside trembled with fear when the French duke of Anjou marched through certain English-held lands in France with an army of two thousand lances,● six thousand foot soldiers armed with pikes and shields, and many others. The people of the castles and towns, much frightened, rushed to surrender. Great criticism of their actions followed. Did they surrender out of fear or out of sympathy for the French? This I do not know.

"The answer is not easy. At the Battle of Poitiers a French knight fled in fear. An English knight caught up with him and said, 'Sir Knight, turn about. You ought to be ashamed thus to fly,' and then took him prisoner. A French squire also ran away. A young English knight pursued him and quite the opposite happened—the frightened squire turned about and captured his pursuer.

"Sir Dana himself was often scared. When he was, he would remember these words, written by a fellow knight and author, Sir Geoffrey de Charny. 'He who puts his trust in his own strength alone will at the last be undone.' Sir Dana knew he was not alone in this world. He put his trust in God, his companions in arms, his family, his friends, sometimes even his enemies—and, yes, in himself.

"He prayed for his cause to be always just. As with most people, sometimes it was and sometimes it was not."

● Medieval for *foolish, crazy, lunatic*
● A lance was one fully equipped knight or squire, supported by three or four servants, soldiers, or archers.